THE ADOLESCENCE

OF

ZHENYA LUVERS

THE
ADOLESCENCE
OF
Zhenya Luvers

by

Boris Pasternak

PHILOSOPHICAL LIBRARY
NEW YORK

Library of Congress Catalog Card No. 61-15246

Printed in the United States of America

CONTENTS

Preface

Boris Pasternak first achieved fame, both in his native Russia and abroad, as a lyric poet. His father was a well-known painter, while his mother was a talented pianist. He studied music for some years, then philosophy at the Universities of Moscow and Marburg. He joined the Cubo-Futurists in 1912, but was only associated with them briefly, and, except for his interest in obscure words and his occasional use of shocking or vulgar imagery, he had little in common with the Futurists. His first collection of poetry, *A Twin in the Clouds*, was published in 1914. He won wide recognition after the First World War with a collection of lyrics called *My Sister Life*, written in 1917 but published only in 1922. With the publication of successive collections, he soon acquired the position of the leading younger poet of Russia. His *Spektorski* (1926) is an attempt at treatment of certain episodes of his own life. As a narrative work, it was somewhat less successful than his lyrics, as were his other narratives, *1905* (1925-26) and *Lieutenant Schmidt* (1926-27), both attempts to celebrate the revolutionary movement in

Russia. Pasternak aims at a personal, lyric verse, and the revolutionary movement is a subject which seems alien to his real interests. His collection *The Second Birth* (1932) frequently employs the Caucasus and its magnificent landscapes as a setting, and these poems, like others by Pasternak, sometimes recall Lermontov's Caucasian poetry.

Though Pasternak's poetry is difficult and at times obscure, he became the favorite poet of Soviet intellectuals, and there is little doubt that he is one of the leading poets of our time. The obscurity of his work, its individualism and concern for personal subjectivity made much of his work unacceptable to orthodox Soviet critics, who attacked him for "formalism" and "alienation from the masses." Apparently driven from original creation by the hostile pressure of his critics, Pasternak turned to translation, producing excellent versions of several of Shakespeare's plays as well as selections from American and Georgian poets. He took advantage of the somewhat more lenient atmosphere of the time of the Second World War to publish two new original collections: *On Early Trains* (1943) and *The Terrestrial Expanse* (1945), which show a certain simplification and greater directness by comparison with his earlier work. But in 1946 the critics launched a new attack, and thereafter he published no poetry except in translation.

As a poet, Pasternak was highly individualistic. Philosophical themes and the contemplation of reality were favorite subjects, along with the more conventional themes of love and nature. Nature in his poetry appears as new and strange; the poet describes her almost animistically as alive, and re-creates for us something of the elemental wonder of a primitive view of the world. But Pasternak's "primitivism" is actually part of a sophisticated but deliberately irrational approach to nature, which he depicted in strikingly rich and novel images. He is unusual as a lyric poet whose poetry tends to be prosaic in its great use of synecdoche and metonymic imagery, of part-whole and object-symbol relations. His metaphors and similes are especially remarkable in their freshness, and he was not in the least afraid to use images of objects which are of a technical nature, or are prosaic or even vulgar. Thus, he compares the guilt of a lover to a skin infection, or the color and feel of fresh air to a bundle of wash taken home from a hospital. Images of sound are particularly striking in his poetry, as when he speaks of the "clatter of winter" or the "rumble of grief."

Pasternak's prose is an extension of his poetry, with the same prosaic quality and the same unexpectedness of imagery. In 1925 he published his only collection of stories, in which appeared the present work, *The Adolescence of Zhenya Luvers*. The story is virtually plotless, full of reminiscences which Pasternak "objectivizes"; a young girl's reactions to the world about her seem to become part of that very world. Another story is *Air Ways* (1925), set against the background of the 1917 Revolution, depicting in a fragmentary and quite unsentimental manner a father's inability to save his illegitimate son, arrested for taking part in a counterrevolutionary conspiracy. But the story as such is less important than its imagery. *Safe Conduct* (1931) is

3

an autobiographical account of the poet's youth and early spiritual development.

Pasternak has been compared to a number of modern poets, including Eliot, Hopkins and Rilke. More than they, however, he is a writer whose subject was a new manner of perception, a manner far more important than what is perceived or what is believed. It is the fresh way of perceiving reality which is original in his work. During the 1920's Pasternak had considerable influence on a number of young Soviet poets, including Tikhonov, Bagritski and Selvinski. But his influence largely waned with the attacks on his work by Soviet critics.

In 1958 a novel by Pasternak, *Dr. Zhivago*, appeared in Italy; subsequently the work was published in English and in many other languages. *Dr. Zhivago* is a lyrical novel of the life of Russian intellectuals during World War I, the Civil War and the early years of the Soviet regime. The hero is a physician and poet who reacts to the tragic happening of history by passive withdrawal and a search for freedom within himself. His love for Lara, the novel's heroine, is a triumphant assertion of life in the face of the logic of historical events; so also is his creative work as a poet. The novel is a symbolic depiction of the spiritual death of Russia, particularly the old Russia of the intelligentsia, in the Revolution; at the end of the book the possibility of regeneration is symbolized by the appearance of Zhivago's daughter Tanya. Marxism and Communism are sharply criticized by the author; to them he opposes a Darwinian conception of life and a Christian philosophy of history which emphasizes individual freedom.

Later in 1958 the Nobel Prize for literature was offered to Pasternak; he at first accepted it, but later rejected it after he had been subjected to a storm of vituperation by Soviet critics. To date (1961) the novel has not been published in the Soviet Union. Pasternak died in 1960 of heart disease.

WILLIAM E. HARKINS

Columbia University.

I

The Long Days

Zhenya Luvers was born and grew up in Perm. Later on, her memories were buried in the many shaggy bearskins of the house, as her little boats and dolls had been earlier. Her father was manager of the Luviewsky Mines and had many customers among the manufacturers of Chusovaya.

The luxuriant, brown-black bearskins were gifts. The white she-bear in the nursery was like a giant, full-blown chrysanthemum. This fur had been especially chosen for "Zhenichka's room." It had been carefully selected, purchased in a store after long bargaining, and brought to the house by a delivery boy.

In the summer the Luvers lived in a country house on the other side of the Kama. In those years Zhenya used to go to bed early, and did not see the lights of Motovilikha. But, one night, the Angora cat, frightened in her sleep, made a violent movement and woke up

7

Zhenya. Suddenly she saw people on the balcony. The alder tree which overhung the balcony railing was iridescent like thick, dark ink. The tea in the glasses was red. The men's cuffs and the cards were yellow and the tablecloth green. It was like a nightmare, but it was a nightmare with a name that Zhenya knew: it was called "a game of cards."

But what was going on, on the other shore of the river, in the far, far distance, she could not recognize; it had no name, no definite color or clear contours. Its billowing movements had something dear and familiar about them; it was no nightmare like the one close by, which murmured in clouds of tobacco smoke and threw fresh, wind-tossed shadows on the reddish beams of the gallery. Zhenya started to cry. Her father came in and explained everything to her. Her English governess turned her face to the wall. The explanation was brief: "That is Motovilikha. You should be ashamed of yourself. Such a big girl! Now go to sleep!"

The girl understood nothing and swallowed a salty tear. She had wanted only one thing, to know the name of the inconceivable: Motovilikha. That night the name explained everything and that night the name still held a real and reassuring meaning for the child.

But in the morning she asked what Motovilikha was and what they made there at night. She learned that it was a factory, that it was owned by the government, that cast iron was made there, and that cast iron was made into. . . . But that did not interest her. She would have liked to know what "factories" were—maybe they were different countries—and who lived in them. But

8

she did not ask this question; indeed, she deliberately refrained from asking it.

That morning she ceased to be the child she had been in the night. For the first time in her life she suspected that there existed phenomena which either kept certain things to themselves or revealed them only to people who could scold and punish, smoke and lock doors with keys. Like this new Motovilikha, for the first time she too did not say everything she thought but kept the essential, basic and disturbing things to herself.

Some years passed. The children were from an early age so used to the absence of their father that fatherhood was linked in their minds with a certain habit of coming seldom to lunch and never to dinner. More and more often they ate and drank, played and shouted, in deserted, solemnly empty rooms, and the coldly formal lessons of their English governess could not replace the presence of a mother who filled the house with the sweet torture of her temper and willfulness as with a familiar electricity. Through the curtains streamed the quiet northern light. It never smiled. The oaken cupboard looked gray, its silverware piled up heavy and severe. The hands of their governess, bathed in lavender water, smoothed the tablecloth. She gave nobody less than his due and had as strong a sense of justice as a feeling for order; her room and her books were always meticulously clean and tidy. The girl who served the food waited in the dining room and went to the kitchen only to fetch the next course. Everything was comfortable and beautiful, but terribly sad.

These were years of distrust and solitude for the girl,

of a feeling of guilt and of what the French would call "*christianisme*"—something that could not possibly be translated "Christianity." Sometimes Zhenya believed that she neither could nor should have things any better; she deserved nothing different because of her wickedness and impenitence. Meanwhile—though the children never became wholly aware of it—the behavior of their parents threw them into confusion and rebellion; their whole beings shivered when the grownups were in the house, when they returned—not *home*, but to the house.

Their father's rare jokes fell flat and sounded mostly out of place. He felt this and sensed that the children noticed it. A tinge of sorrowful confusion never left his face. When he was irritated, he became a complete stranger, from the instant he lost his self-control. One is not touched by a stranger. But the children took care never to answer him impudently.

For some time now, however, he had been insensitive to criticism from the nursery, which was aimed at him dumbly from the eyes of the children. He no longer noticed it. Invulnerable, impenetrable, and somehow pitiable, *this* father was far more terrible than the irritated father, the stranger. He disturbed the little girl more than the boy.

The mother confused both children. She showered them with caresses and gifts and passed whole hours with them when they least desired it, when it oppressed their childish consciences because they felt that they did not deserve it. They did not recognize themselves in the tender pet names that her maternal instinct lavished on them.

10

And often, when an exceptional calm ruled their souls, when they did not feel like criminals, when everything mysterious that shies away from revelation, and is like the fever before the rash, had left their consciences, they saw their mother also as a stranger, who pushed them aside and became angry without reason. For instance, the mailman would come, and the children would bring a letter to her. She would take it without thanking them. "Go to your room!" The door closed. They hung their heads in silence and were plunged into long, disconsolate doubts.

At first they had sometimes cried; then, after a particularly violent outburst of anger on their mother's part, they became frightened. In the course of the years this fear turned into a concealed hostility which struck ever deeper roots in their hearts.

Everything that came to the children from their parents seemed to come at the wrong moment, from far away, as if produced not by them but by mysterious, unknown causes. It smelled of a great distance and was like the groaning of the folding screens when they went to bed.

These circumstances molded the children. They never knew this, for even among grownups there are few who know and feel what shapes them, forms them and links them with one another. Life lets but a few people in on what it is doing to them. It loves its work too much and talks while it works only with those who wish it success and love its workshop. No one has the power to assist it, but anyone can disturb it. How can one disturb it? Quite simply. When a tree is left to grow undisturbed, it grows crooked, grows only roots or wastes itself upon a single leaf, for it forgets that it must take the universe as its model and, once it has brought forth one out of a thousand possible things, it continues to bring forth the same thing a thousand times.

To ensure that no dead branches remain in the soul to hinder its growth, and that man does not inject his stupidities into the creation of his immortal being, many things are provided to divert his trivial curiosity from life, which does not like to work in his presence and avoids his scrutiny in every possible way. Among these diversions are all genuine religions, all generally accepted ideas and all human prejudices, including the most brilliant and interesting psychology.

The children had already gotten over their first illnesses. Concepts such as punishment, retribution, reward and justice had already, in childish form, penetrated their souls, diverted their consciousness and let life do anything with them that it thought necessary, essential and good.

2

Miss Hawthorne would not have left, except that Mrs. Luvers, in one of her motiveless outbursts of tenderness toward the children, spoke sharply to the governess apropos of nothing very important and the English-woman disappeared. Shortly thereafter she was imperceptibly replaced by a thin Frenchwoman. Later on, Zhenya could recall only that the Frenchwoman looked like a fly and that nobody liked her. Her name deserted Zhenya completely, and she could not say under what syllables and sounds it was to be found. All she remembered was that the Frenchwoman had shouted at her, and then taken a pair of scissors and cut the blood-stained spot from the bearskin.

It seemed to her that she was now always being scolded and that she would never again understand a page of her favorite book—it became so blurred before her eyes, like a textbook after a heavy lunch.

The day dragged terribly. Her mother was not at home, but that did not bother Zhenya. In fact, it seemed to her that she felt happy about it.

The long day soon passed into oblivion over the forms of the *passé* and the *futur antérieur,* the watering of the hyacinths and walk in Sibirskaya and Okhanskaya Streets. It was so forgotten that she felt the length of the following day—the second endless day of her life— only toward evening, when she was reading by lamp-light and the dragging action of the story lulled her into a hundred lazy thoughts. And when she later thought of the house in Osinskaya Street, where they lived at the time, it always looked to her as it looked at the end of this second long day—a day without end. Outside it was spring. In the Urals, spring is sickly and matures painfully; then, in the course of a single night, it makes a wild and stormy break-through, after which it enters upon a wild and stormy growth.

The lamps only emphasized the emptiness of the

evening air. They gave out no light. Like spoiled fruit, they swelled from the hydophilia inside them, which blew up their bloated shades. They were located where they should be: standing in their proper places on the tables and suspended from the stucco ceiling. But the lamps had fewer points of contact with the room than with the spring sky, to which they were as close as a water glass to a sickbed. Their souls were in the street, where the gossip of servant girls buzzed over the wet earth and individual waterdrops gradually turned to ice and grew rigid for the coming night. Out there the lamps disappeared in the evening. Their parents were away, but their mother was expected that day—on that longest day or the next one. Yes, perhaps she would return quite suddenly. That, too, was possible.

Zhenya went to bed and discovered that the day had been long for the same reason as the previous one. At first she wanted to get a pair of scissors and cut out the spots from her nightgown and the bed sheet; but then she decided to take the French governess' powder and whiten the spots with it. She was reaching for the powder box when the governess came in and struck her. All sinfulness became concentrated in that powder. "She powders herself! That's the last straw. I suspected as much for a long time."

Zhenya burst into tears because the governess had struck her and scolded her; because she was upset because she had not committed the crime of which she was accused; because she knew that she had done something much uglier than the governess suspected. She had to—she felt this deep in her stunned conscience,

14

in her very calves and temples—she had to conceal this, without knowing how or why, but somehow and at any price. Her aching joints moved heavily, as if under a hypnotic compulsion. This tormenting, paralyzing compulsion was the work of her body, which hid from the girl the meaning of the whole frightening process, which behaved like a criminal and forced her to regard this bleeding as somthing disgusting and abominably evil. *"Menteuse!"* She could only deny everything, obstinately conceal what was worse than anything else and lay somewhere between the disgrace of illiteracy and the shame of making a row in the street. She could only shiver, clench her teeth, suppress her sobs and lean against the wall. She could not throw herself into the Kama; it was still cold and the last floes of ice were still moving down the river.

Neither she nor the Frenchwoman heard the doorbell in time. The tension in the house was absorbed by the thick, brown-black bearskins, and when her mother came in, it was already too late. She found her daughter in tears and the governess livid with anger. She demanded an explanation. The Frenchwoman quickly explained that—no, not "Zhenya" but *"votre fille"*—"your daughter" had been powdering herself, that she had seen her doing it and had suspected her for a long time. The mother let her talk herself out; her own horror was genuine—the girl was not quite thirteen. "Zhenya! My God, how far have you gone?" (In that moment, these words had a special meaning to the mother, as though she already knew that her daughter was on the wrong path, that she herself had failed to intervene in

15

time, and that now her own daughter had already sunk this low.) "Zhenya, tell me the whole truth, or else it will be even worse. What have you done—" Mrs. Luvers wanted to say "done with the powder box," but she said—"with this thing?" And she took the "thing" and waved it in the air.

"Mama, don't believe Mam'selle. I have never . . ." and she began to sob. But her mother heard unrepentant tones in this crying that were not there at all. She felt guilty and became frightened; she believed that she could put everything right and "take pedagogical and rational measures," even if it went against her maternal instinct. She decided not to yield to compassion. She would wait until the girl's stream of tears, which hurt her deeply, had stopped.

She sat on the bed and stared with a quiet, empty look at the edge of the bookshelf. She smelled of an expensive perfume. When Zhenya regained her self-control, her mother questioned her again. Zhenya, with tearful eyes, looked out the window and swallowed. Outside the ice floes drifted by, probably with a crunching noise. A star sparkled. And there was the dull blackness of the desolate night, supple and cold, but dark. Zhenya looked away from the window. Her mother's voice sounded a note of warning impatience. The Frenchwoman stood against the wall, an image of strictness and concentrated pedagogy. Her hand lay on the wrist band of her watch—the gesture of a military aide. Zhenya cast another glance at the stars and the Kama. She was resolved, in spite of the cold, in spite of the drifting ice—she would throw herself in. She lost herself in her words, in her terrible, incoherent words, and told her mother about *that*.

Her mother let her finish only because she was startled to see how much of the child's heart and soul went into her account. From the first word, everything became clear to her. No—she knew even as the girl took a deep breath, before she started her story. The mother listened happily, lost in love and tenderness toward this thin little body. She wanted to throw her arms around her daughter's neck and kiss her. But, no—pedagogy! She rose from the bed and removed the bedspread. She called her daughter to her, and caressed her hair slowly, very slowly and tenderly. "My good child . . ." she managed to say, then went hastily to the window and stood with her back to the other two.

Zhenya did not see the Frenchwoman. Her tears— her mother—filled the whole room. "Who makes the bed?" the woman asked. It was a senseless question. The girl shrank into herself. She felt sorry for Grusha. Then her mother said something in French, a language with which she was familiar—but these words were harsh and incomprehensible. Then she said to Zhenya, in a completely different voice, "Zhenichenka, go into the dining room, my child. I'll be there right away. I'll tell you about the wonderful country house Papa and I have rented for you—for us all—for the summer."

The lamps became familiar to her again, as in the winter, at home, with the family, warm, eager, loyal. Her mother's marten fur was thrown carelessly over the blue tablecloth. "Good. Stay at Blagodat. Wait till the end of Holy Week, when—" She couldn't read the rest, the telegram was folded. Zhenya sat down on the edge of the sofa, tired and happy. She sat there relaxed and satisfied, just as she was to sit half a year later on the edge of the yellow bench in the corridor of the Yekaterinburg High School when she passed her Russian oral exam with the highest grade and was told that she could "go now."

The next morning her mother told her what to do when it happened again, that there was nothing more to it, that she need not be afraid, that it would happen again and again. She never called "it" by name and explained nothing to her, but she added that hereafter she intended to teach her daughter herself since she wouldn't be going away any more.

The Frenchwoman was dismissed for negligence; she had been with the family only a few months. When the cab came for her and she walked down the front steps, she met the doctor who was just coming up. He acknowledged her greeting in a most unfriendly manner and said no word of farewell to her. She guessed that he already knew everything, made a sour face and shrugged her shoulders.

The servant girl, who had ushered in the doctor, lingered outside the door, and so the noise of the footsteps and of the reverberating stones remained longer than usual in the corridor where Zhenya stood. And when later she thought of her awakening puberty, she always called back this memory: the loud echo of the busy morning street which hesitated on the doorstep and then gaily entered the house; the Frenchwoman, the servant girl and the doctor; two sinners and a confidant, cleansed and purified by the clear sound of shuffling steps.

April was warm and sunny. "Wipe your feet, your feet," shouted the empty corridor from one end to another. The furs were laid away for the summer. The rooms were cleaned, transformed; they seemed to sigh in relief. The black alder tree laughed and frolicked the whole day, the long exquisitely painful day, primping itself untiringly, in all the corners, in all the rooms, in all the winter windows, in mirrors, in glasses of water, in the blue garden air. And the honeysuckle washed itself with sighs and swallows. The chattering in the yard lasted the full twenty-four hours. The days announced that the night had been vanquished, and repeated day in and day out, in swelling tones, which made one feel drowsy, that there would be no more evening and that they would let no one sleep. ". . . Your feet, your feet . . ."

But the children glowed. They came home drunk with freedom, with a sound in their ears that made them miss the meanings of words, and they were in a rush to finish eating as quickly as possible, to push their chairs back noisily and run out again into this day, which broke impetuously into evening—into this day where drying wood gave out crackling noises and the blue of the sky twittered shrilly and the earth glittered moistly, like melted butter. The border between the house and the yard was wiped out. The cleaning rag had not washed away all traces of its work. The floors were covered with a light, dry wax and they squeaked underfoot.

Their father brought home sweets and other wonderful things. In the house everything was wonderful. The sweetmeats announced with a damp rustle their emergence from the tissue paper; the little white packets, soft as gauze, gradually acquired color and became more and more transparent as the paper was peeled off layer by layer. Some looked like almond milk drops, others like splashes of blue water color, still others like solidified "cheese tears." Some were blind, sleepy or dreamy; others sparkled insolently like the frozen juice of blood-red oranges. One hardly bear touch them. They were perfect on the frothy paper that had secreted them as plums secrete their cloudy juice.

The father was unusually tender to the children and often accompanied their mother into town. They would return together and seemed happy. But the most important thing of all was that both were quiet, eventempered and friendly, and even if Mother occasionally gave Father a playfully reproachful look, she seemed to be drawing peace from his small, not very attractive eyes and pouring it out upon the children from her own large, beautiful ones.

One day their parents got up very late. Then they decided—nobody knew why—to have breakfast on the steamer that lay in the harbor, and they took the children along. Seryozha was allowed to try the cold beer. They all had such a good time that they breakfasted again on the steamer.

The children hardly recognized their parents. What had happened to them? The girl was confused with happiness and believed it would stay like this forever. The children were not even disappointed when they were told they would not spend the summer in the country house. Soon afterward their father went away. Three gigantic yellow traveling trunks with solid iron bands appeared in the house. . . .

3

The train left late at night. Mr. Luvers had gone ahead a month earlier and had written that the apartment was ready. Now they rode in carriages to the railway station, going at a slow trot. They knew they were getting close to the station from the color of the pavement, which became greasy-black and from the light of the street lamps which was reflected from the dark rails. At the same moment they saw the Kama from the viaduct, while below them ran a pitch-black chasm, rumbling with the noise of freight cars. It shot off like an arrow, and far, far at the other end, seemed to lose itself frighteningly under the twinkling pearls of distant signal lights.

The night was windy. The contours of the houses flew away like phantoms, staggering and shaking in the turbulent air. There was the smell of potatoes in the air. Their coachman broke out of the snakelike line of bouncing cars and carriages in order to get ahead of them. They saw, from a distance, the cart with their luggage; they passed it. Ulyasha shouted something from the cart to her mistress, but the rattling of the wheels drowned out her voice; she was jolted from side to side and her voice bounced up and down too.

Zhenya felt no sadness of departure, for these night noises, the darkness and the freshness of the night air were quite new to her. In the far distance the darkness deepened. Behind the harbor buildings, the lights of boats and the shoreline itself wavered and seemed to dip into the water. On the Lyubimovsky wharf chimneys, warehouses, roofs and ship decks stood out, a sober blue color. Roped barges stared up at the stars. "There is a rathole," thought Zhenya.

Porters in white uniforms surrounded her. Seryozha was the first to leap from the carriage. He looked around and seemed surprised that the cart with their luggage had already arrived; the horse tossed his head, his collar rising like the coxcomb of a strutting rooster; he leaned against the cart and sat down on his hind quarters. And here, all through the ride, Seryozha had been trying to estimate how far the cart lagged behind!

The boy, intoxicated with the thought of the journey before him, stood there in the white shirt of his high school uniform. For both children the journey was something new and unknown, but the boy already knew and loved such words as "station," "engine," "railroad siding," and "express train," and the collection of sounds called "class" had for him a bittersweet taste. All this interested his sister, too, but in her own way, without

22

the boylike cataloguing of information which was part of her brother's excitement.

Suddenly their mother stood like a wall beside them. She herded the children into the railway restaurant. From there she strode through the crowd, looking proud as a peacock, straight to the man who was, for the first time, addressed as the "stationmaster," and who would often be referred to later under different circumstances.

The children were overcome by fits of yawning. They sat by one of the windows, which were so grimy, decorated with painted designs, and so gigantic that they looked like enormous officials, made of glass, to whom one should take off one's cap. Zhenya saw behind the glass not a street, but a vast room, gloomy and more solemn than the room reflected in the water carafe before her. Engines entered this room, came to a halt and shut out the light with their great bulk. But when they left the room, it became clear that it was no room at all; there was the sky behind the tall columns and on the horizon a hill, with wooden houses toward which people walked; roosters crowed there perhaps, and possibly the water carrier had just been there and had spilled some water.

It was just a provincial railway station, without the crowds and noise of a big city terminus. Travelers came here early and waited a long time. It was a quiet station, with peasants moving about or sleeping on the ground among hunting dogs, crates, machinery packed in straw and unpacked bicycles.

The children lay now in their upper berths. The boy fell asleep immediately, while the train was still standing. It grew light and the girl noticed gradually that the coach was clean and cool. And she was beginning to notice . . . but then she was already asleep. . . .

He was a very fat man, reading a newspaper and rocking back and forth. As soon as one looked at him one became aware of the rocking, which like the sun flooded and permeated everything in the compartment. Zhenya looked down on him from above with that lazy clarity with which one regards an object after rousing from a good sleep. Especially if you remain in bed until the decision to rise comes of itself, without any intervention of the will, and all your thoughts are clear and unforced. She looked at the man and wondered how he had entered the compartment and when he had had the time to wash and dress. She had no idea what time it was. She had just wakened so it must be morning. She examined the man, but he could not see her because the upper berths were steeply inclined toward the wall. In addition, he hardly ever looked up or sideways from his newspaper, and when he did look up, their eyes did not meet. He either saw only her mattress or— But she quickly picked up her stockings and put them on. Mama sat in the other corner of the compartment. She had already dressed and was reading a book. But Seryozha was nowhere to be seen. Where could he be? She yawned pleasurably and stretched. She suddenly became aware that it was dreadfully hot, and she looked over the heads of her mother and man toward the half-open window. "But where is the earth?" her soul cried within her.

What she saw could not be described. The swaying

forest of hazelnut trees, through which the train was winding, became a sea, the world, anything one wished it to be. The sunlit, murmuring forest ran down sloping hills, the trees becoming smaller, denser and gloomier, until it fell away steeply into a black emptiness. And what hung on the other side of the chasm was like a greenish-yellow storm cloud, twisted and convoluted, but frozen, turned to stone. Zhenya held her breath and suddenly felt the speed of this limitless, unself-conscious air, and saw that the storm cloud was a great mass of earth, that it had the name of a famous mountain, which rolled down like thunder and was hurled with sand and rocks into the valley, that the hazelnut forest knew the name and whispered it ceaselessly, here, there, everywhere.

"Is this the Urals?" she asked the whole compartment and leaned out of the berth.

She spent the rest of the journey glued to the window in the corridor, leaning out. She was greedy for this new experience. She discovered that it was much more beautiful to look backward than forward. Majestic acquaintances wrapped themselves in mist and disappeared in the distance. After a brief separation, while over the rhythmic clatter and rattle of the couplings a cold draft hit the back of your neck and a new marvel emerged right before your nose, you discovered them again. The mountain panorama stretched itself out and grew ever larger. Some mountains became darker, others were suddenly sunlit; some were obscured, others disappeared into darkness. They met and separated, they fell and rose. All this moved slowly in a circle, like the stars, with the cautious gyrations of giants, missing disaster by a hair's-breadth, ever worried about the preservation of the earth. These complicated motions were accompanied by a steady and powerful echo that was inaudible to human ears, but which was aware of everything. It watched them with eagle eyes, dark and dumb. It held a grand parade. Thus are the Urals built, built and rebuilt.

She returned for a moment to the compartment and shut her eyes to the dazzling light. Her mother was talking and laughing with the fat man. Seryozha was sliding back and forth on the red plush seat, holding on to a leather strap fastened to the wall. Her mother spat out the last fruit pulp into her hand, swept away the pips that had fallen on her dress, leaned over lithely and tossed the debris under the seat. The fat man, contrary to all expectation, had a hoarse, cracked voice. He obviously suffered from asthma. Her mother introduced Zhenya to him, and he gave her a tangerine. He was comical and probably good-natured. Time and again he raised his pudgy hand to his mouth when he spoke. His voice rose, suddenly sounded strained and was abruptly cut off. It turned out that he lived in Yekaterinburg, had traveled all over the Urals and knew them very well. When he took his gold watch out of his waistcoat pocket, held it close to his nose and put it back, Zhenya saw that he had good-natured fingers. Like all fat men he did things with an air, as though he were giving them away, and his hand sighed all the time, as if offered for a kiss, and swayed softly in the air, as if it were bouncing a ball on the ground. "It will soon be here," he murmured and turned his squinting gaze away from Seryozha, at whom he had just glanced, and smiled broadly.

"You know, the frontier post between Asia and Europe. Asia is written on it," bubbled Seryozha. He slid quickly from his seat and ran into the corridor.

Zhenya didn't understand what he meant, and when the fat man tried to explain it to her, she, too, ran out to wait for the signpost; she was afraid that she had already missed it. In her bewitched head the "frontier of Asia" became a fantastic borderline, like the iron bars which establish a danger zone between the public and a cage full of mountain lions, a zone as black as night and smelling of danger. She waited for this post as for the raising of the curtain on the first act of a geographical tragedy of which she had heard fabulous things from people who had seen it; she felt triumphant because now she would see it with her own eyes.

Meanwhile, the monotony which had driven her back to the grownups in the compartment, returned. The gray alders, which they had been passing for half an hour, seemed endless, and nature appeared to be making no preparations for what was about to happen. Zhenya was annoyed with boring, dusty Europe, which lazily delayed the appearance of the miracle. And how startled she was when, almost simultaneously with Seryozha's wild cry, something like a tombstone flitted by the window, turned its other side to them and carried off the longed-for, fairy-tale name deep into

the pursuing alders. As if by previous agreement, countless heads shot out of the windows of the compartments
of all classes, while a cloud of dust swirled around the
train, which was whizzing down a slope. It had already
traveled dozens of miles into Asia, but kerchiefs still
fluttered over darting heads, and clean-shaven and
bearded faces still looked out as they flew along on
clouds of sound, past the dusty alders which had been
European a short time ago but were now Asiatic.

4

A new life began. The milk was not brought to the
house and into the kitchen by a milkwoman; Ulyasha
brought it in every morning in two pails attached to a
yoke. The rolls, too, tasted different from those at Perm.
The pavements looked like marble or alabaster, with a
wavy, white shine. The stones dazzled one in the shade
like icy suns and greedily swallowed the shadows of
the elegant trees which grew overhead, melting and
dissolving them. One had a different feeling walking
the streets here, which were light and broad, tree-lined
as in Paris, Zhenya would say, parroting her father.

He had said that the day they arrived. It was a beautiful, clear day. Having breakfasted before coming to
the station to meet them, he did not take the midday
meal with them. He merely sat down with them, spread
out his napkin, and brought them up to date. He un-
buttoned his waistcoat, his hero's breast swelling stiffly

and powerfully. He said Yekaterinburg was a beautiful European town, then rang the bell for the course to be taken away and a new one brought in. A girl in white came noiselessly over unknown paths from unknown rooms, a brunette, all stiffly starched pleats and ruffles. Mr. Luvers addressed her in the formal second personal plural. She smiled at the lady and the children as if they were old acquaintances. She was given certain instructions for Ulyasha, who was in the unknown kitchen, where there surely must be a window through which one could see something new: perhaps a bell tower or a street or birds. And having put on her oldest clothes and unpacked, Ulyasha would surely ask this new girl many questions, in order to find her way around the kitchen—such as in which corner the hearth stood, whether the same as in Perm or in another.

Mr. Luvers told Seryozha that it was only a few steps to the high school, it was quite near by. They had seen it on their way to the house. Their father drank some mineral water, swallowed and continued: "Didn't I show it to you? You can't see it from here, perhaps from the kitchen." He thought it over. "But only the roof." He took another swallow of mineral water and rang the bell.

The kitchen was cool and light, just as Zhenya had imagined it in the dining room; the blue-white tiles sparkled, and there were two windows, arranged as she had imagined they would be. Ulyasha threw something over her exposed arms. They heard children's voices from outside and saw people walking on the roof of the high school and just the top of a scaffolding. "Yes, they are making repairs," explained their father as they returned noisily, in single file, to the dining room. They passed through the already known but yet unexplored corridor, which Zhenya vowed to explore more thoroughly tomorrow when she had unpacked her schoolbooks, hung up her clothes and attended to a thousand other things.

"Excellent butter," said their mother as she sat down. The children went into the schoolroom, which they had already briefly inspected on their arrival, caps still on their heads. "What is this Asia?" Zhenya reflected aloud. But Seryozha failed to understand what he surely would have understood at any other time, for until now they had lived in the same world. He ran to the map on the wall, drew his hand up and down the ridge of the Urals and looked at his sister, who he thought should be convinced by this demonstration. "They agreed upon a natural frontier, that's all."

She thought of today's noon hour, already so far in the past. It was incredible that this day, which already contained so much—the same day that was *now* in Yekaterinburg and was still here—was not yet over. At thought of all this withdrawing to a certain distance, yet still maintaining its breathless order, she felt a strange weariness in her soul, a feeling that the body has on the evening of a day heavy with work. It was as if she had helped in moving these heavy, beautiful things and had overstrained herself. And somehow convinced that *they*—the Urals—were *there,* she turned and ran into the kitchen, passing through the dining room, where there were now fewer dishes but the "excellent" iced butter on wet maple leaves and the irritating mineral water still remained.

The high school was being repaired and shrill swallows tore the air, as a seamstress tears linen with her teeth, while below—she leaned out of the window—a coach gleamed before the open coachhouse, sparks flew from a whetstone, and there was a smell of leftover food, so much better and more interesting a smell than that of freshly prepared food. It was a long-drawn, melancholy odor, as in a book. She forgot why she was standing there and failed to notice that her Urals were not in Yekaterinburg. Then she noticed that it was gradually growing darker and that the people on the floor below were singing, probably while doing housework. Perhaps they had washed the floors and were now spreading the bast mats with their warm hands. She also heard water spilling into pails below, and yet how quiet it was all around. She heard a faucet dripping and the call, "Well, now, miss!" but she was still shy of the new girl and she didn't want to hear her. And now—she thought her thought to its end—the people below must be saying, "The people on the second floor have arrived." Then Ulyasha came into the kitchen.

The children slept deeply the first night and they woke up, Seryozha in Yekaterinburg, Zhenya in Asia, as it seemed to her with a strange certainty. White alabaster ornaments were playing on the ceiling.

It was still summer when it started. It was explained to her that she would go to high school, and this only pleased her. It was not *she* who called the tutor into the schoolroom, where sunlight stuck so fast to the distempered walls that, when evening came, the tenaciously clinging day could be torn off only with bloodshed. She had not called for him when he arrived, accompanied by her mother, to be introduced "to his future pupil." Did she by any chance wish that soldiers must always exercise in the noonday heat, giant, panting soldiers, with sweat like the red stuff that comes from the faucet of a damaged water main? She did not wish that a violet storm cloud, which knows more of guns and artillery than of white shirts, white tents and even whiter officers, should ease off their boots. Had she by any chance prayed that two things, a bowl and a napkin, should be combined like the carbon elements of an arc lamp and produce a third thing that turned in a flash into steam: the idea of death? It was while looking at the emblem of barbershops that this idea had first come to her. And did the red barricades, with the notice of "No Standing Here," become, perhaps, with her consent a place of hidden secrets, and the Chinese turn into something terrible that terrified Zhenya personally? Not everything weighed so heavily upon her soul. Much was beautiful, for instance her forthcoming attendance at high school. But when everything was *explained* to her, life ceased to be a poetic whim; it billowed around her like a gloomy, dark tale and became hard, factual prose. Dull, painful and dim, like a state of perpetual sobering up, the elements of the day's routine fell into her awakening soul. They sank to the bottom, real, hard and cold, like sleepy tin spoons. There, in the depths, the tin began to melt, became lumpy and turned into pressing thoughts.

5

The Belgians came often to tea. That's what they were called. That's what their father called them when he said, "The Belgians are coming today." There were four of them. The beardless one came rarely and was less talkative. Sometimes he came alone, by accident, in the middle of the week and chose an ugly, rainy day for his visit. The other three were inseparable. Their faces, scented and cool, reminded one of fresh pieces of soap, just unwrapped. One of them had a thick, fluffy beard and soft, chestnut-brown hair. They always came with Mr. Luvers from some conference. Everyone in the house liked them. They spoke as if they were sprinkling water on the tablecloth—noisily, briskly, with sudden twists that nobody expected. Their jokes and anecdotes, clean and satisfying, were always understood by the children.

Noise was everywhere, everything flashed—the sugar bowl, the nickel coffeepot, the strong white teeth, the heavy linen. With Mrs. Luvers they joked pleasantly and courteously. As her husband's colleagues, they knew how to restrain him when he made ponderous replies to their allusions to people only they, as experts, really knew. Haltingly and long-windedly, in bad French, Mr. Luvers told stories of contractors, of *"références approuvées"* and of *"férocités,"* that is *"bestialités, ce qui veut dire en russe,* embezzlements, in Blagodat."

The beardless one, who had been eagerly learning Russian for some time, often tried himself out in this new territory, but it wouldn't bear his weight as yet. It was improper to laugh over the French sentences of their father, whose "*férocités*" were embarrassing to the children, but the laughter that drowned out Negarat's experiments in Russian seemed to be justified by the situation itself.

His name was Negarat. He was a Walloon from the Flemish part of Belgium. They recommended Dikikh, Zhenya's tutor, to him. He wrote down the address in Russian and made very comic pictures of complicated letters like "*yu, ya, yat!*" They looked as if they were double, these letters, as if they stood straddle-legged. The children let themselves kneel on the leather seats of the chairs and lean their elbows on the table—everything was allowed when the Belgians were there, everything was higgledy-piggledy. The letter "*yu*" was not a "*yu*" but a figure too. They all shouted and shook with laughter. Evans hit the table with his fist and wiped away his tears. Their father walked up and down the room, shaking and red-faced, saying over and over, "No, I can't go on," and crumpled his handkerchief in his hand. Evans added fuel to the fire: "*Faites de nouveau! Commencez!*" Negarat timidly opened his mouth, as if fearful of stuttering, and considered how to pronounce the Russian "*yery,*" still as unexplored as the colonies along the Congo. "*Dites: uvy-nevy-godno,*" their father proposed to him in a hoarse, choking voice. "*Ouivoui, nievoui. . . .*" "*Entends-tu? Ouvoui, nievoui—ouvoui, nievoui—oui, oui—chose inouie—charmant!*" the Belgians shouted, rocking with laughter.

The summer was gone. The exams were passed, some even with distinction. The cold, transparent noise in the school corridors flowed as if from a well. Here everybody knew each other. The leaves in the garden turned yellow and gold. The school windows tormented themselves with their bright, dancing reflection. Half of milk glass, they darkened and their lower parts shook. The upper panes quivered in a blue cramp. Bronze maple brandies furrowed their cold clarity.

She had not expected that all her excitement would turn into such a lighthearted joke. Divide so many ells and inches by seven! Was it worth while to learn all these *"dols, zolotniks, lots,* pounds and poods?"* The grams, drams, somples and ounces, which always seemed to her like the four ages of the scorpion? Why does one write *"polezno"* with an *"e"* and not with a *"yat"*? The answer was so difficult for her only because she strained her imagination to envisage why a *"yat"* should suddenly appear in the middle of a word, although it made the spelling look so wild and unkempt. And her coffee-brown school uniform, cut out but still held together with pins, was fitted to her for hours. And her room already held many new horizons: school satchel, pen case, lunchbox and a remarkably repulsive eraser.

II

The Stranger

The little girl was wrapped from head to knee in a thick woolen muffler and ran about the yard like a chicken. Zhenya wanted to go to the Tartar girl and speak to her. And at that moment a casement window flew open. "Kol'ka!" Aksinya called. The child, who looked like a peasant's bundle with felt boots hastily attached, ran into the porter's quarters.

To take schoolwork into the yard always meant brooding so long over some comment on a rule that it lost all sense, with the result that one had to return home and start all over again. On the very doorstep, the rooms began to weave their spell, with their special twilight, their coolness and their always surprising familiarity; it emanated from the furniture standing in its proper place for all time. The future could not be foreseen, but it could be seen when one stepped into the house from outside. Here its plan was made evident —the distribution of those forces to which it would be subjected. And there was no dream blown in by the movement of the air in the street that the spirit of the house did not swiftly dissipate at the very door of the entrance hall.

This time it was Lermontov. Zhenya opened the book in the middle and bent back the covers till they met. When Seryozha did this at home, she always protested against this "ugly habit." But outside it was something else again.

Prokhov set the ice machine on the ground and entered the house. When he opened the door to the Spitsenskys' hallway, the devilish yelps of the general's short-haired dogs could be heard. The door shut with a bang.

Meanwhile, the Terek roared like a lioness with a shaggy mane and roared on, as was only proper. Zhenya was wondering whether all this took place on the "back" or on the "backbone." She was too lazy to look it up and "the golden clouds from faraway southern lands" had barely accompanied the Terek to the north, when she collided with Prokhov on the doorstep of the general's kitchen, a pail and bast mop in hand.

The orderly put down the pail, leaned over and, taking the ice machine apart, started to wash it. The August sun pierced the leaves and settled on the soldier's loins. Blazing-hot, it penetrated the coarse uniform cloth and soaked it through like turpentine.

The yard was large, with many meaningful corners. The paving in the center had long gone unrepaired; thick, curly grass had long since overgrown the stones. In the hours after lunch the grass smelled like a sour medicine, like a hospital, in the noonday heat. One end of the yard, between the porter's lodge and the coach-house, bordered on somebody else's garden.

Zhenya went to the place where the firewood was stacked. She wedged a flat log under the ladder which leaned against it to prevent it from slipping, and sat, uncomfortable and strained, as if in a game, on one of the middle rungs. Then she got up, climbed higher, put the book on the top step and attempted to deal with the "Demon." Then she discovered that it was more comfortable sitting below and made her way down, leaving the book on the woodpile, without noticing it—because it was just then that she discovered something on the other side of the garden that she had never suspected. As if under a spell, she stood open-mouthed.

In the strange garden there were no bushes, and the ancient trees, stretching their lower branches through the foliage as into dark night, sheltered the garden beneath, which lay in a constant, solemn but airy twilight, from which it never emerged. The branches were forked, painted violet by the weather, covered with gray lichens, and left open a view of an empty, little-used street on the other side of the garden. There a yellow acacia stood. Its leaves were now dry, shrunken and falling.

Transformed by the dusky garden from this world into another, the empty side street shone like an event in a dream, very bright, sullen and still, as if the sun, with spectacles on its nose, were rummaging in a crowfoot.

What then made Zhenya open her mouth in wonder? A discovery that interested her far more than the people who helped her make it.

Was there a small shop. . . ? Behind the garden gate . . . In such a street . . . "The happy ones" . . . She envied the unknown women. They were three.

They were black, like the word "nun" in the song. Three symmetrical necks bowed under round hats. The outermost one, half-concealed by a bush, was leaning on something and seemed to be asleep. The other two, nestling tightly against her, were also asleep. The hats were blue-black, they shimmered in the sun and then went out, like fireflies. They were entwined with black crepe. At this moment, the unknown women turned their heads and looked in another direction. Something at the far end of the street had obviously attracted their attention. They stared that way for a minute, as one stares in the summer when the light dissolves a second and draws it out, when one blinks and has to protect one's eyes with a hand—they stared for a moment, and then sank back into their former state of sleepy immobility.

Zhenya wanted to go into the house, but she missed her book and could not remember immediately where she had left it. Then she went to fetch it and when she reached the woodpile she saw that the unknown women had moved and were about to leave. They walked in Indian file to the garden gate. A small man with the peculiar gait of the lame followed them. He carried under his arm a gigantic album or atlas. So that was what had occupied their attention when they were looking over each other's shoulders and she had thought they were asleep! The strangers walked through the garden and disappeared behind the farm buildings. The sun set. Zhenya reached for her book and slipped on the logs. The woodpile woke up and moved as if it were alive. A few logs slid down and fell onto the grass with a quiet bump. This was the sign, like the night-watchman's tap with the door knocker. The evening was born. From the other side of the river the air whistled an old tune.

The yard was empty. Prokhov had finished his work and gone outside the gate. Out there the melancholy strumming of a soldier's balalaika now glided closely, very closely, over the grass. Above it danced a thin swarm of mosquitoes. The strumming of the balalaika grew still thinner and fainter. It sank deeper toward the earth than the insects, but it never quite fell into the dust; lighter and airier than the mosquito swarm, it rose, twinkling and dissolving in peaceful harmonies.

Zhenya returned to the house. "Lame," she thought of the unknown man with the album, "lame but a gentle-man without crutches." She went in by the back door. The yard smelled sweetly and obtrusively of camellias. "Mama has a regular drugstore, a mass of little blue bottles with yellow caps."

She walked slowly up the stairs. The iron railing was cold. The steps creaked in response to her dragging pace. Suddenly a strange thought entered her mind. She took two steps at a time and stopped on the third. She discovered that there had existed for some time an inexplicable likeness between her mother and the porter's wife. It was quite inexplicable. She stood still. It is, she thought, like when one says, "We are all people" or "We are all baptized with water" or "Fate makes no difference. . . ." She pushed away a fallen bottle with the tip of her foot, and it fell below on the dusty mat without breaking. She thought, "It is something quite universal, something that all men have in common." But why, then, was there no likeness between herself and Aksinya? Or between Aksinya and Ulyasha? This seemed all the stranger to Zhenya because two more different persons could hardly be imagined. Aksinya had an earthy quality, like a vegetable garden, which recalled a knobby potato or a swollen gray-green pumpkin, but Mama . . . Zhenya smiled at the mere thought of the comparison.

But it was Aksinya who gave the tone to this pressing comparison. It was she who had the superiority. The peasant woman lost nothing by it, but the lady lost something. For a second Zhenya had a crazy thought. It seemed to her that something simple and rural had entered into the essence of her mother, and she imagined her saying "ap'l" instead of "apple" and "wo'k" for "work." Maybe the day will come, she thought, when she wears her new beltless silk morning dress and sails in like a ship and greets us with peasant words. The corridor smelt of medicine. Zhenya went in search of her father.

2

New furniture was bought. Luxury came into the house. The Luvers bought a coach and kept horses. The coachman's name was Davlecha.

42

Rubber-tired wheels were quite a novelty at the time. When they went for a ride, everything turned and stared after the coach: people, fences, chapels and roosters.

When the coach, out of respect for Mrs. Luvers, started off at a walking speed, she shouted after them: "Don't go too far, only to the turnpike and back. And look out when you go down the mountain!" The pale sun, which reached her on the doctor's veranda, glided further along the street, till it reached the nape of Davlecha's freckled neck and warmed him so that his skin contracted pleasantly.

They drove over the bridge. The conversation of the planks sang out, cunning, full and clear; it was fixed for all time, forever locked in the chasm below and always in her memory, at noon and in her sleep.

Vykormish stamped up the mountain and tried his strength on the steep, unyielding pavement. He stretched and pulled and heaved; he looked like a wriggling locust and, humbled by his unnatural effort, he suddenly became beautiful, like the creature that by its very nature is meant to jump and fly. It seemed as if he couldn't bear it any longer, his wings flashed angrily, he soared. Really! The horse pulled in, then threw his forelegs high and dashed in a brief gallop through a fallow field. Davlecha shortened the reins and curbed the horse. A thin, shaggy dog barked at them stupidly. The dust was the color of gunpowder. The road turned sharply to the left.

The black road ended at the fence of a railway warehouse. The air felt restless. The sun came slantingly through the bushes and veiled a group of strange small shapes in feminine clothes. The sun bathed them in a white light which appeared suddenly, pouring like liquid lime from a pail overturned by a shoe and ran like a wave over the ground. Bands of sunlight covered the road. The horse moved at a walking pace.

"Turn left," Zhenya ordered. "There is no road there," Davlecha replied and pointed out a red fence with his whip. "A dead end."

"Then stop. I want to look around."

"There are our Chinese."

"Yes, I see." Davlecha noticed that the young lady no longer wanted to converse with him. He sang out a long-drawn "prrrrrr" and the horse, its whole body shaking, stopped as if it had taken root. Davlecha whistled softly and encouragingly to help the horse do what was necessary.

The Chinese ran across the street, giant loaves of rye bread in their hands. They were dressed in blue and looked like women. Their naked heads were crowned by knots on top, which seemed to be twisted in place by handkerchiefs. Some of them hesitated, and one could study them closely. Their faces were dark with dirt, like copper oxidized by poverty. Davlecha took his tobacco pouch from his pocket and began to roll a cigarette. At that moment several women appeared on the corner toward which the Chinese were moving. Probably they also were going to fetch bread. The Chinese who stood in the road guffawed and walked toward the women. They moved back and forth as if their hands were tied together with ropes. Their rocking motions were emphasized by the fact that from neck to ankles they looked poured into gowns cut like those of acrobats. There was nothing frightening about them, and the women did not run away, but stood there laughing.

"Davlecha, what are you doing?"

"The horse pulls; it doesn't want to stay here."

Davlecha beat the horse a few times with the reins, then drew them tight and let them out again. "Quiet! You'll overturn the coach!"

"Why do you beat him?"

"I have to."

And only when the sly Tartar was in an open field and the shying horse had quieted down and, swift as an arrow, had removed his young lady from the shameful scene, did Davlecha take the reins into his right hand and put his tobacco pouch, which he had been holding all the while, back under his coat tails.

They returned by another route. Mrs. Luvers saw them coming, probably from the doctor's window. She came to the threshold at the very moment when the bridge, which had told them its whole tale, resumed it under the water carrier's cart.

3

The entrance examination at the high school brought Zhenya together with a girl called Lisa Defendov, who had picked rowanberries along the way and brought them with her to school. The daughter of a choir leader had to repeat her French exam. Eugenia Luvers was seated in the empty seat next to her. And so they became acquainted as they sat side by side repeating the same sentence: "*Est-ce Pierre qui a volé la pomme? Oui, c'est Pierre qui a volé . . . etc.*"

The fact that Zhenya had been tutored at home proved no handicap to the friendship of the girls. They met often. The visits, however, were one-sided, thanks to certain views held by Zhenya's mother: Lisa could come to see her friend, but Zhenya was forbidden, for the time being, to go to the Defendovs.

The intervals between their meetings did not keep Zhenya from attaching herself quickly to her friend. She loved Defendova—that is to say, she played a passive role in their relationship. She became Lisa's "pressure gauge," watchful and easily upset. All of Lisa's remarks about her classmates, whom Zhenya did not know, roused in her a feeling of impending rage and bitterness. She was depressed and sad. These were the first attacks of jealousy. Without reason, and solely on the basis of her distrust, Zhenya was convinced that Lisa was playing a game with her, that outwardly she made a show of sincerity but privately laughed about everything that marked her as a Luvers, sneering behind Zhenya's back at school and at home. But Zhenya found that this was the way it had to be, that it was in the nature of her attachment. Her feeling sprang from the powerful desire of an instinct that knows no self-seeking and can do but one thing: suffer for the sake of its idol and burn itself out when it really feels for the

46

first time. Neither Zhenya nor Lisa influenced each other permanently. Zhenya remained Zhenya; Lisa remained Lisa; they met and separated—the one deeply moved, the other completely untouched.

The father of the Akhmedianovs dealt in iron. In the year between the birth of Nazzedin and Smagil he suddenly became rich. Thereafter Smagil was called Samuel and the father decided to give his sons a Russian education. The father overlooked not one peculiarity of the way of life of a *"Carin,"* a gentleman, and after ten years of eager imitation he had in every respect overshot his goal. The boys did excellently—that is, they adhered strictly to the model their father held up to them, and the brashness of their father's ambition remained with them, noisy and destructive, so that they were like two circling flywheels left to the mercy of the power of inertia.

In the fourth class the Akhmedianov boys were merely fourth-class pupils. They were made up of broken pieces of chalk, cheating, buckshot, rattling school benches, vulgar swearwords and red-cheeked, snub-nosed self-confidence. Seryozha befriended them in August. By the end of September the boy no longer had a character of his own. This was in the nature of things. To be a typical high school boy, and the type he later becomes, means to join the camp of the Akhmedianovs. And Seryozha wanted nothing more passionately than to be a typical high school boy. Luvers placed no obstacles in the way of his son's friendships. He noticed no change in the boy, and had he noticed any, he would have ascribed it to adolescence. Besides, he had more serious worries. He had suspected for some time that he suffered from an incurable disease.

4

She was sad, but not for his sake, although everybody agreed how terribly annoying and awkward it must be. Negarat was too wise even for her parents, and all that the parents felt about foreigners transmitted itself indistinctly to the children, as to spoiled pets. Zhenya was sad only because things were no longer the same, because only three Belgians were left, because there was no longer so much laughter.

On the evening Negarat told Mama he had to go to Dijon to do his military service, she was sitting, it so happened, at the table.

"Then, you must be very young," their mother said and there was sympathy in her voice. He sat with drooping head, and the conversation came to a dead stop. "Tomorrow we put in the winter windows," Mrs. Luvers went on, and asked Negarat whether she should shut the window. He said it wasn't necessary, in his country there were no winter windows.

Their father came in soon afterward. He, too, offered expressions of regret when he heard the news. But before he uttered his laments, he asked in astonishment, "Dijon? Then you are not a Belgian?"

"Yes, I am a Belgian, but a French citizen." And Negarat told the story of the emigration of his "two old folks" in such an interesting way, as if he were not their son, but with as much warmth as if he were reciting from a book about strangers.

"Excuse my interrupting you," said their mother. "Zhenya, please shut the window. Vika, tomorrow the windows must be sealed. Now please continue. This uncle of yours was a real scoundrel. Did he *literally* say that under oath?"

"Yes." And he resumed his story. Then he began talking about his own affairs—the papers he had received yesterday by mail from his consulate. He noticed that Zhenya failed to grasp what it was all about, but was trying hard to understand. Carefully, in order not to wound her pride, he began to explain in detail what military service was all about.

"Yes, yes, I understand. I do understand," Zhenya repeated gratefully and mechanically. "But why must you go so far away? Can't you become a soldier here, and drill where everybody else drills?" In her imagination she saw the drill meadows that could be seen from the monastery hill. "Yes, yes, I understand. Oh, yes," she reassured him.

But the Luvers, who sat by, taking no part in this exchange, felt that the Belgian was simply stuffing the girl's head with unnecessary detail and threw in lazy, oversimplified comments of their own. Then suddenly the moment came when Zhenya felt sorry for all those who, a long time ago or very recently, had been like Negarat, who had said good-by and taken an unknown route, which had been decreed by fate, in order to become soldiers here at Yekaterinburg, a completely strange place to them. The man had explained everything to her so well. Nobody had made it so clear to her before. The wall of indifference, the crumbling wall of concrete, fell away from before the picture of the white tents; the regiments disappeared and turned into a crowd of real people in soldiers' uniforms, for whom she felt personally sorry the moment the new meaning given to them brought them to life, stripped them of their exotic glamour, and turned them into fellow creatures.

They said good-by to Negarat. "I am leaving part of my books with Tsvetkov. He is the friend I have told you so much about. Please keep reading them, Madame. Your son knows where I've been living; he often visits the landlord's family. I will pass on my room to Tsvetkov. I will tell him to expect to hear from you."

"He should come visit us sometime. Tsvetkov, did you say?"

"Yes, Tsvetkov."

"He should certainly drop in. We'd like to meet him. I knew the family as a child. . . ." And she noticed her husband standing before Negarat, his hands grasping the lapels of his tight-fitting coat and distractedly awaiting the moment when he could make final arrangements for tomorrow with the Belgian. "He should come, but not right away. I will let him know when. Now please take this book—it is yours. I haven't finished it, but I cried over it, and the doctor advised me to stop reading altogether. To avoid excitement." And again she glanced at her husband, who stood with his head down, collar crackling, cheeks inflated, as if investigating with great interest whether he really had shoes on both feet and whether they had been properly polished. "Yes, that's how life is. Please don't forget your walking stick. I do hope we'll see each other again."

"Of course, we shall. Friday. What day is it today?" Negarat became anxious, the way all those who leave become anxious.

"Wednesday. Is it not Wednesday, Vika? Yes, Wednesday."

"*Ecoutez.*" Finally their father spoke. "*Demain. . . .*" and taking Negarat's arm, they walked downstairs together.

5

They talked as they walked along. Zhenya from time to time had to break into a light trot in order not to be left behind and to keep up with Seryozha. They walked very fast, her coat sliding back and forth, because she had her hands in her pockets and was steering herself with her arms in order to get up more speed. The thin ice broke with a crunch under their rubbers. They were going to buy a gift for Mama to give their departing friend. And they talked as they walked along.

"They took him to the railway station?"

"Yes."

"But why did he sit in the straw?"

"What do you mean?"

"In the cart. Up to his legs."

"I told you already—because he is a prisoner, a criminal."

"Are they taking him to jail?"

"No, to Perm. There is no criminal court here. Watch out for your feet."

They had to cross the intersection, passing the workshop of a coppersmith. The workshop doors had stood open all summer and Zhenya was used to seeing the intersection in a state of friendly commotion, set off by the open jaws of the workshop. All through July, August and September carts stopped here for repairs and blocked the street. Peasants, mostly Tartars, stood around, buckets and pieces of broken, rusty gutter pipe strewn everywhere. The blazing, persecuting sun turned the crowd into a gypsy encampment and painted the Tartars with gypsy colors. It sank into the dust at about the hour when hens were killed behind the neighbors' fences. The cart frames, freed from their animals, let their shafts with their greased plates drop into the dust.

The same buckets and the same scraps of metal still lay in confused disorder, now powdered with hoar frost. But the doors were tightly shut against the cold, as on a holiday. The intersection was empty, and only the familiar odor of stuffy gas, which flowed with a shrill screech from an air valve, reached Zhenya's nostrils and clung to them as a cheap fruit wine clings to the palate.

"But is there a prison administration in Perm?"

"Yes, the criminal department. . . . I think we go this

way. . . . The prison is in Perm because it is the provincial capital. Yekaterinburg is only a district capital—a hole."

The narrow street led them past houses standing on their own plots of land; it was paved with red bricks and lined with bushes. Streaks of watery sunlight lay on the little street. Seryozha tried to stamp his feet as loudly as possible. "If you tickle this thorn bush in the spring, when it blossoms, its petals will go pop as if they were alive."

"I know."

"Are you ticklish?"

"Yes."

"Then you must be nervous. The Akhmedianovs say that's so if you're ticklish."

They walked on, Zhenya trotting, her coat swinging back and forth, Seryozha with his naturally long stride. They came upon Dikikh when they stopped at a small turnstile at the end of the narrow street. They saw him coming out of a shop half a block away. Dikikh was not alone. He was followed out of the shop by a little man who tried to conceal a limp as he walked. It seemed to Zhenya that she had seen him before. They passed each other without greeting, the other two moving off in a diagonal direction. Dikikh hadn't noticed the children; he wore high rubbers and kept lifting his hands with fingers outstretched. He seemed not to agree with something his companion was saying and was trying to prove it with his ten fingers. Where had she seen the limping man? A long time ago. But where? Probably in Perm, in her childhood.

"Stop!" Something was bothering Seryozha—he dropped to his knees. "Wait!"

"Does it hurt?"

"Yes. These idiots, they can't even drive a shoe nail properly."

"Well..."

"Wait, I can't find it . . . I know the lame man . . . Well, thank God!"

"Tom?"

"No, thank God. There's a hole in the shoe lining, that's what it is. I can't help it now. Come on. Wait, I must brush my knees. All right, let's go.

"I know him. He's staying with the Akhmedianovs. A friend of Negarat. Remember? I told you about him. He entertains people. They drink all night and there is light in the windows. You remember—when I stayed the night with the Akhmedianovs, on Samuel's birthday. He is one of those. You remember now?"

She remembered. She realized that she had been mistaken, that she hadn't seen the lame man for the first time in Perm as she had thought. But she still felt as if she had seen him there. With this feeling nagging her, she explored her memory for everything she could remember from Perm, walking silently behind her brother. She made certain movements, took hold of something, made a turn and found herself in semi-darkness among counters, boxes, shelves, servile bowings . . . and Seryozha was talking.

The bookseller, who also dealt in all kinds of tobacco, didn't have the book they asked for. But he tried to mollify them by assuring them that the Turgenev they ordered had been sent out from Moscow and was on the way and he had just this minute spoken of it to Mr. Tsvetkov, their tutor. His ingeniousness and his mistake amused the children; they said good-by and left the store empty-handed.

As they were going out, Zhenya asked her brother, "Seryozha, I always forget. Do you know the street you can see from our woodpile?"

"No, I've never been there."

"That's not so. I've seen you there myself."

"On the woodpile? No, you—"

"No, not on the logs, but in the street behind the Cherep-Savich garden."

"Oh, you mean that! Yes, that's right. Behind the garden, way back, beyond the sheds and firewood. Wait a minute. Is that our yard—that yard? Ours? That's good. When I walk that way I always feel like climbing on the woodpile, and from there onto the storehouse. I've seen a ladder there. Is it really our yard?"

"Seryozha, will you show me the way there?"

"What? But if that's our yard, why should I show it to you? You yourself—"

"Seryozha, you don't understand again. I mean the street, but you're talking about the yard. Show me how to get there. Will you show me, Seryozha?"

"I don't understand you again. We'll go there right now."

"Really?"

"Yes. And the coppersmith . . . at the corner?"

"Also the dusty street . . ."

"Yes, that's just what you're asking for. And the

Cherep-Savich garden is at the end on the right. Don't loiter, or we'll be late for dinner. We're having crayfish today."

They spoke of other things. The Akhmedianovs had promised to show him how to solder a samovar. And in answer to her question about what solder was made of, it was a metal, like tin, quite dull. You used it to solder tins and repair kettles and the Akhmedianovs could do all sorts of things like that.

They had to hurry crossing the road or a coach would have held them up. Therefore they forgot, Zhenya her question about the little-used side street and Seryozha his promise to show it to her. They passed the door of the coppersmith's shop, and when they breathed in the warm, fatty exhalation that is given off during the cleaning of copper handles and candlesticks, Zhenya suddenly remembered where she had seen the lame man and the three others and what they had done. A minute later, she knew that the Tsvetkov of whom the bookseller had spoken was the limping man.

6

Negarat left in the evening. Their father accompanied him to the train. He came back from the station late at night, and his arrival set off a loud, long-lasting hubbub in the porter's lodge. Somebody came out with lanterns and called somebody else. It was raining buckets, and the geese, whom someone had let out, were cackling frantically.

A growly, shaky morning began. The wet, gray street bounced as if it were made of rubber. The nasty rain splashed mud, the coaches bounced on the paving stones and spit mud at pedestrians in overshoes.

Zhenya was returning home. Reverberations of the night's row in the yard could still be heard in the morning; she was not allowed to use the coach. She had said she wanted to buy some hemp seed and went to see her friend on foot. But halfway there, she realized that she could not find her way from the business quarter to the Defendovs' street and turned back. Then it also occurred to her that it was too early, Lisa would still be at school. She was wet to the skin and shivering. The wind grew stronger. But it grew no lighter. A cold, white light fell into the street and lay like leaves on the wet pavement. At the end of the square, behind the three-branched street lamp, dull, huddling clouds hurried in panic toward the town.

The man engaged in moving was either very untidy or impractical. The furniture from his modest workroom was not properly loaded on the cart, but was simply arranged in the same way it had stood in the room, and the castors on the armchairs which peeped from under the white covers glided over the planks as over a dancing floor with every jolt of the cart. The covers shimmered snow-white although they were soaked through. They hit the eye so glaringly that everything else took on their brightness: the paving stones pounded by the water, the shivering pools of water under the fences, the birds flying from the stables, the pieces of lead and even the fig tree in its bucket, which rocked to and fro and bowed clumsily from the cart to all the hurrying passers-by.

The cart was grotesque, and automatically attracted attention. A peasant was walking beside it. The cart listed sharply to one side and moved forward at a walking pace. And over all its groaning plunder hung the wet, leaden word "town"; it brought to life in the girl's head a number of images as fleeting as the cold October brilliance which flew along the street and fell upon the water.

"He will catch a cold when he unpacks his things," she thought of the unknown owner. And she imagined a man, any man, as he moved about, staggering and with uneven steps, arranging his belongings in his new lodging. She saw vividly in her imagination his gestures and movements, especially the way he took a rag, limped around the bucket and wiped the hoar frost from the leaves of the fig tree. And she saw him catching the sniffles, the shakes, a fever. He would certainly catch a cold. Zhenya imagined all this vividly. The cart rumbled down the hill, toward the Isset. Zhenya had to turn left.

It probably came from the heavy steps. The tea rose and fell in the glass on the bedside table. The slice of lemon floating in the tea rose and fell. The sun streaks on the carpet rocked to and fro. They swayed like columns, like rows of syrup bottles in shops with signboards showing a Turk smoking a pipe.

Showing a Turk . . . smoking . . . a pipe. Smoking . . . a pipe . . .

It probably came from the heavy steps. The sick girl went back to sleep.

Zhenya became ill the day after Negarat's departure, the day she learned on her walk that Aksinya had given birth to a boy, the day she imagined, when she saw the furniture cart, that its owner was threatened with rheumatism. For two weeks she lay in fever, covered with perspiration, sprinkled all over with red pepper which burned her and glued her eyelids and the corners of her mouth together. The perspiration drove her to distraction, and the awareness of shapeless statues mingled with the feeling of being stung. As if the flame that caused her to swell had been poured into her by a summer wasp. As if the sting, a thin gray bristle, had remained stuck in her and she tried to get it out in all possible ways—sometimes from her violet cheekbones, sometimes from the inflamed shoulder that groaned under the nightdress, sometimes from other places.

Then her convalescence started and the feeling of weakness permeated everything. This feeling of weakness abandoned itself, at its own peril, to a strange geometry that was peculiar to it and which produced a slight giddiness and nausea.

It started, for example, on the bedspread. The feeling of weakness piled up on the bedspread rows of gradually growing, empty rooms, which in the shivery twilight rapidly began to take the shape of a square which formed the basis of this mad game with space. Or else it loosened band after band from the wallpaper pattern, which made unique patterns before her eyes, as if they were swimming on oil; one pattern took the place of another, their dimensions grew slowly and steadily, like all these hallucinations, and tormented her. Or else the feeling of weakness tortured the girl with a sense of measureless depths which betrayed their bottomlessness instantly with the very first trick they played on the dancing floor. The bed sank quietly into the abyss and the girl sank with it. Her head was like a lump of sugar which is thrown into a yawning, empty chaos, dissolves and disappears.

It came from the heavy steps. The slice of lemon rose and fell. The sun on the wallpaper rose and set. . . .

Finally she woke up. Her mother came in and congratulated her on her recovery. Zhenya had the impression that her mother could read other people's thoughts. When she woke up, she had heard similar words—the congratulations of her own hands, feet, elbows and knees, which she had accepted, stretching herself out. Their greeting had wakened her. And now Mama, too. It was a strange reunion.

The people in the house came and went, sat down and got up again. They asked questions and received answers. Some things had changed during her illness, others had remained unchanged. The former didn't touch her, the latter gave her no peace. Her mother had obviously not changed. Neither had her father. But certain things *had* changed: herself, Seryozha, the distribution of light in the room, the quiet of the other people and some other things.

Had it snowed? Only a little and it melted immediately. There was only a little frost, it was hard to say how things looked, naked, without snow. She hardly noticed whom she asked and what she asked. The answers seemed like a pressure forced on her. The healthy people came and went. Lisa came. There was an argument. Then it occurred to everyone that you can get measles only once and they let her in. Dikikh visited her. She hardly noticed which answers came from whom. When everybody was eating lunch and she was alone with Ulyasha, she remembered how everybody in the kitchen had once laughed over her silly questions. She would be careful now not to ask about such things. She would ask only sensible, relevant questions, in the tone of a grownup. She asked whether Aksinya was pregnant again. The girl rattled the spoon when she took away the glass. "But, my dear child, let her have a rest. She cannot keep on being pregnant, Zhenichka." She ran out and left the door only half-closed. The whole kitchen rumbled as if the shelves had fallen with all their dishes, and laughter was followed by a loud hooting. It flew toward the cleaning woman, flared up under her hands, clattered and rattled as if a quarrel had passed into blows. Then somebody came and shut the forgotten door.

What is this? Will it thaw again? Then she would have to go by coach again today, for it wasn't yet possible to go by sleigh. With a chilly nose and hands stiff with cold, Zhenya stood a long time by the window. Dikikh had just left. He had been dissatisfied with her. How can one learn one's lessons when outside the roosters crow and the sky rumbles and when the rumble ceases, the roosters crow again? Black, dirty clouds like a naked cave. The day thrusts his snout at the window-pane like a calf in a steaming barn. Will spring ever come again? But since lunch a blue-gray frost encircles the air like a hoop, the sky becomes hollow and collapses, the clouds breathe audibly, with a whistling sound, the hurrying hours, flying northward toward the winter darkness, tear the last leaves from the trees, flatten the lawns, break through the chinks, pierce the breast. The mouths of northern storms yawn black behind the house, laden with November. But it is still October.

It is still October. No one can remember such a winter. People say the winter seeds will freeze. They fear a famine. It was as if somebody winked and drew a circle with a magic wand around chimneys, roofs and the starlings' boxes. There will be fog, snow and hoar frost. But until now, neither the one nor the other. The empty, hollow-cheeked twilight longs for them. It strains the eyes. The early lanterns and the lights in the houses hurt the earth, as one's head is hurt by a long waiting, when one stares into the distance with dim eyes. Everything waits tensely, the firewood is already piled in the kitchen, for two weeks the clouds have been filled to the brim with snow, the air is pregnant with darkness. But when will the wizard who casts a spell over everything the eye can see and binds it within a magic circle pronounce his incantation and call forth the winter whose breath already steams just outside the door?

How had they neglected it? Really, nobody had bothered about the calendar in the schoolroom. She tore

off the leaves. Childish! But still, it was not August 29!
"That's good," Seryozha would have said. A red-letter
day. The decapitation of John the Baptist. The calendar
let itself be lifted easily from the nail. She tore off the
leaves because she had nothing else to do. She grew
bored and soon ceased to be aware of what she was
doing, but from time to time she murmured to herself:
"The thirtieth. Tomorrow is the thirty-first."

The words "She hasn't been outside for three days"
reached her from the corridor, snatching her out of her
daydreams. She observed how far her aimless work had
taken her—all the way to the day of Mary's Sacrifice. Her
mother touched her hand. "Zhenya, I ask you, please
tell me . . . "

She didn't hear what followed, as if it hadn't been
said. As if in a dream, Zhenya interrupted her mother,
and asked her to say, "The decapitation of John the
Baptist."

Her mother repeated these words uncomprehendingly.
She didn't say "Battist." It was Aksinya who said that.

The next moment Zhenya was wondering about herself. What was it? Who had driven her to it? Where did
it come from? Had she, Zhenya, asked this? How could
she think that Mama—how fantastic and improbable!
Who had invented all this?

Her mother was still standing there, not trusting her
ears. She stared at Zhenya with large eyes. This outburst
embarrassed her. This request sounded as if Zhenya
wanted to make fun of her. But there were tears in her
daughter's eyes.

Her dark foreboding came true. On the pleasure ride
she noticed clearly that the air was growing milder and
that the rattling of the hoofs sounded muffled. Even before she had lit the carriage lamps, dry flakes whirled
through the air. They weren't over the bridge before
the individual flakes vanished and the snow fell as a
thick, closely packed mass. Davlecha climbed down from
the driver's seat and put up the leather hood. For
Zhenya and Seryozha it became dark and cavern-like.
They would have liked to rage like the wild storm. They
only noticed that Davlecha was driving home because
they again heard the bridge under Vykormish's hoofs.
The roads could no longer be recognized—they were
gone. The night closed in suddenly, the town looked
like a crazy thing, moving countless thick, pale lips.
Seryozha knelt on the seat, leaned out of the carriage
and ordered the coachman to drive to the vocational
school. Zhenya was lost in rapture when the secrets and
charm of winter came to her with the echo of Seryozha's
words through the muffled air. Davlecha shouted back
at him that they had to return home so as not to exhaust
the horse; the master and mistress were going to the
theater and the horses must be harnessed to the sleigh.
This reminded Zhenya that her parents were going out
tonight and they would be left alone in the house. She
decided to sit cozily by the lamp till late into the night
reading *Tales of Murr the Tomcat,* which were not intended for children. She would sneak the book out of
Mama's bedroom. And chocolate—she would read and

eat chocolate, while listening to the howl of the wind through the streets.

The snowstorm was already very intense. The sky shook, and white kingdoms and countries fell—numberless, secret and terrible. Nobody knew where they came from and it was clear that they had never in their lives heard of earth. These blind, midnight countries would cover the earth, without seeing it or knowing it. There was a terrible intoxication about these kingdoms, a devilish fascination. Thinking about them, Zhenya swallowed the wrong way and choked for a moment. The swirling air shook everything in its path, and in the far, far distance the fields howled mournfully, as if they were being whipped. Everything was confused. The night threw itself upon the fields, raging through its tangled gray hair, which she cut down and blinded. Everybody out riding shouted that the road could no longer be recognized. Shouts and echoes vanished without meeting and died away, lifted above different roofs by the rampaging wind. The snowstorm.

In the corridor they stamped their feet a long time and shook the snow out of their white, ruffled furs. And how much water flowed from their rubbers onto the checkered linoleum! Eggshells lay on the table, the pepper box had been taken from its stand and not replaced, and pepper lay sprinkled over the tablecloth, the spilled yolks and an opened tin of sardines. Their parents had already eaten their evening meal, but they were still sitting in the dining room and urged the children, who had turned up late, to hurry. They did not scold them, for they themselves had eaten earlier than usual because they were going to the theater. Their mother was uncertain whether she wanted to go or not, and sat there looking depressed. Looking at her, Zhenya realized that she herself was anything but happy.

Finally she opened the silly but rather sad book, and came back into the dining room to ask where the nutcake was. Her father looked at her mother and said nobody was forcing them to go and that they would probably do better to stay home.

"No, of course we'll go," said her mother. "I must have diversion, the doctor said so."

"Well, let's make a decision."

"Where is the nutcake?" Zhenya asked for the second time and was told that she ought to eat something else first—one didn't start with nutcake. However, it was in the cupboard. As if Zhenya were a stranger in the house and didn't know family habits, added her father. Then he turned to her mother and repeated, "Let's make a decision."

"I have decided. We're going." Her mother smiled sadly at Zhenya and went out to dress. Seryozha broke his egg with a spoon. Hastily, like a very busy man, he reminded his father that the weather was rough, that there was a snowstorm, he should remember that; then he laughed. Something embarrassing was happening to his thawed-out nose. He wriggled in his chair and pulled a handkerchief out of his school uniform pants. He blew his nose the way his father had taught him—"without hurting your eardrums"—and said, "We saw Negarat's friend on our way."

"Evans?" the father asked absent-mindedly.

"We don't know that man," Zhenya put in heatedly.

"Vika!" called a voice from the bedroom. Their father got up and went out.

At the door Zhenya collided with Ulyasha, who was carrying a lighted lamp. Soon afterward she heard a door closing nearby. That would be Seryozha going to his room. Today he had surpassed himself—his sister liked it when the Akhmedianovs' friend behaved like a real schoolboy, when it could be said of him that he was wearing a school *uniform*.

Doors opened and shut. Rubbers stamped out. Finally, the master and mistress were gone. . . .

The letter said she had never been touchy, and "if you want something, ask for it, as before," and when the "dear sister," laden with greetings and good wishes, had distinguished her from her numerous relatives, Ulyasha, who was called "Juliana" in the letter, thanked the young lady, turned down the lamp, took the letter, the ink bottle and the rest of the greasy paper and went out.

Zhenya returned to her homework. She kept on dividing the number and put down one dividend after the other. There was no end in sight. The fraction in the quotient rose and rose.

"Suddenly the measles return," went through her head. "Today Dikikh said nothing about the infinite." She felt that she had felt this way earlier today—she'd rather have slept or cried—but she didn't recall what it was about or when it happened for she couldn't think clearly any more. The howling outside the window was dying down. The snowstorm was gradually tapering off. Decimal fractions were something quite new to her.

There was not enough room on the right. She decided to start again at the beginning, to write smaller, and this time check every term. The street became quiet once again. She was afraid she had forgotten the number she had "borrowed" from the next number and she couldn't keep the product in her head. "The window won't run away," she thought and cast threes and sevens into the bottomless quotient. "I will hear them in time. It's quiet now. They won't come in that quickly. They are wearing their furs and Mama is pregnant. I have it now—3773 is repeated. One can either copy it or cross it out." Suddenly she remembered what Dikikh had told her today: "You needn't keep them, you can simply leave them out."

She got up and went to the window. It had cleared. Separate snowflakes sailed out of the black night. They glided toward the street lamp, swam around it and disappeared, to be replaced by others. The streets glittered, a carpet of snow for a sleigh ride. The carpet was white, radiant and sweet like the gingerbread in the story. Zhenya stood at the window and studied the circles and figures that Andersen's silver snowflakes formed around the lamp. She stood there for quite a while and then went to Mama's room to get *Murr the Tomcat.*

She entered without light. One could see without it, for the coachhouse roof threw a reflected brilliance into the room. Beneath the high ceiling the beds froze and glittered. The smoke-gray silk lay where it had been carelessly thrown. The small blouses gave out an oppressive odor of armpits and calico. There was a smell of violets, and the cupboard was blue-black like the night outside and like the dry, warm darkness in which this frozen brilliance moved. A brass knob on the bed shimmered like a lonely pearl. Another one was extinguished by a sheet thrown over it. Zhenya squeezed her eyes together; the brass knob separated itself from the bed and swam to the wardrobe. Then she remembered why she had come. With book in hand, she walked to one of the windows. The night was star-bright. Winter had come to Yekaterinburg. She looked down into the yard and thought of Pushkin. She decided to ask her tutor to assign her an essay on *Eugene Onegin*.

Seryozha tried to gossip with her. He asked, "Did you put on perfume? Give me some, too." He had been nice all day, so rosy-cheeked, but she thought an evening like this might never come again and she wanted to enjoy it alone.

Zhenya returned to her room and started on the *Tales*. She read one and started another. She was so absorbed she didn't hear her brother going to bed in the room next door. A strange game took possession of her face, quite without her knowing it. Her face twisted sideways, like a fish; she pouted her lower lip; and her pupils, glued rigidly to the book as if by a spell, refused to look up, for they were afraid to find *it* behind the chest of drawers. Then she suddenly nodded to the lines as if she gave them her assent—just as one gives approval to a deed and is pleased about the way things have turned out. She read more slowly when she reached the descriptions of the lakes and threw herself head over heels into the night scenes illuminated with Bengal lights. In one passage, a man who got lost shouted, waited for an answer and heard only the echo of his own voice. She suppressed a cry and had to cough. The un-Russian name "Myra" freed her from her spell. She put the book aside and thought: "So this is winter in Asia. What do the Chinese do on such a dark night?" Her eyes fell on the clock. It must be a terrible feeling to be in this darkness with Chinese. She looked at the clock again and became alarmed. Her parents might come back at any minute. It was nearly twelve. She laced up her shoes and hurried to return the book to its place.

Zhenya sat up in bed with wide-open eyes. No, it couldn't be a thief—there were many people. They stamped through the house and talked as loud as in daylight. Suddenly somebody cried out as if he were being murdered, something was dragged along the floor, chairs were overturned. It was a woman's cry. Slowly Zhenya recognized the voices, every one except that of the woman. An incredible running back and forth began. Doors banged. Then a distant door shut, followed by a stifled cry, as if somebody had stuffed something into the woman's mouth. But the door opened again, and a searing, scourging whine shuddered through the house. Zhenya's hair stood on end: the woman was her mother; she had *done* it. Ulyasha was wailing. She also heard the voice of her father, but only once and not again. She heard Seryozha being pushed into a room, and he roared, "Don't you dare to lock me up!" Then, just as she was, barefoot, wearing only her nightgown, she dashed into the corridor, almost colliding with her father. He was wearing his overcoat and shouted something to Ulyasha as he ran. "Papa!" She saw that he was running from the bathroom with a jug of water. "Papa!"

"Where is Lipa?" he shouted in a totally unfamiliar voice. He spilled water on the floor and disappeared through a door. When he came out again a moment later, in his shirt sleeves and without his waistcoat, Zhenya found herself in Ulyasha's arms and didn't hear his words, uttered in a desperate, heart-rending whisper.

"What's wrong with Mama?"

Instead of a reply Ulyasha repeated over and over, "No, no. It cannot be. Zhenya dear, go to sleep, cover yourself up, turn over and lie on your side. A-ah, God! No, no, dear!" she repeated, covered Zhenya up like a small child and went out. It cannot be, but she didn't say *what* could not be, and her face had been wet and her hair disarrayed. Three doors away, a lock clicked behind her.

Zhenya lit a match to see whether it would soon be dawn. It was only one o'clock. She was astonished. Had she really slept only one hour? The hubbub in her parents' room continued. A loud groaning rose and fell. Then, for a moment, an endless, eternal silence. Hurried footsteps and muffled voices broke the silence. A bell rang once, then again. Then words, arguments, orders— so many that it sounded as if the rooms were lit by voices, as a table is lighted by a thousand fading candelabra.

Zhenya fell asleep. She slept with tears in her eyes. She dreamed that there were visitors. She counted them but always miscalculated. Every time there was one person too many. And every time the same horror seized her when she recognized that the extra person wasn't just anybody: it was Mama.

One couldn't help it, one had to feel happy about the small, sunny morning. Seryozha thought of games in the yard, of snowballs, of snowfights with the neighbors' children. Tea was brought to them in the schoolroom, and they were told that there were floor polishers in the dining room. Their father came in. It was soon clear that he knew nothing about floor polishers. He really knew nothing about them. He told them the true reason for the changes in their routine. Their mother was ill. She needed quiet. Ravens flew, with far-echoing caws, over the street, shrouded in white. A small sleigh glided by, pushing its horse forward. The animal was not yet used to the new harness and kept losing the beat.

"You'll go to the Defendovs. I've arranged everything. And you, Seryozha—"

"Why?" Zhenya interrupted.

But Seryozha had guessed why and forestalled his father. "So that you don't catch the infection," he instructed his sister. But the street outside made him restless. He ran to the window as if someone had called to him. The Tartar who came out of the house in his new clothes looked as stately and as highly adorned as a pheasant. He wore a lambskin cap, and his bare sheepskin coat had a sheen warmer than morocco leather. He waddled and rocked slightly, probably because the raspberry-red pattern on his white boots ignored the natural structure of the human foot. These patterns

72

moved arbitrarily; they cared little whether the objects beneath them were feet, teacups or roof tiles. But the most interesting thing of all—at this moment, the weak groaning that came from the bedroom grew louder and their father went into the corridor, forbidding them to follow him—the most interesting thing of all was the tracks he left on the smooth snow with his sharp, narrow boot tips. These tracks, looking as if they had been carved, made the snow appear even whiter and silkier.

"Here's a letter. You'll give it to Mr. Defendov. Personally. Do you understand? Now get dressed. You'll be taken there immediately. Go to the rear entrance. Seryozha, the Akhmedianovs are expecting you."

"Really?" the boy asked rather mockingly.

"Yes. Get dressed in the kitchen!"

Their father spoke distractedly and accompanied them slowly to the kitchen, where their furs, caps and mittens were heaped like a small mountain on a stool. The winter air blew in from the stairs. "Ah-yoch!" The frozen call of flying sleighs hung in the air. Since they were in a hurry, they missed their coat sleeves once or twice. Their clothes smelled of closets and sleepy fur.

"What are you doing? Don't put it on the edge of the table or it will fall off. Well, how are things?"

"She's still groaning." The chambermaid lifted her apron, leaned down and threw some small logs into the flames of the rumbling kitchen stove. "That's not my affair," she said with annoyance and went out of the room.

In a dented black pail lay yellowed prescriptions and broken glass. The towels were soaked with fresh as well a clotted blood. They seemed to blaze, as if they could be trod out like flaring embers. Only water boiled in the pots. Everywhere stood white crucibles and mortars of unusual shape, as in a drugstore. Little Halim was breaking up ice blocks in the hallway.

"Is there much left from the summer?" asked Seryozha.

"We'll soon have new ice."

"Here, give it to me. You're not doing it right."

"What do you mean, not right? I have to break it into little pieces. For the bottles."

"Well, are you through?"

While Zhenya ran once more through the rooms, Seryozha went out onto the steps and beat the icy railings with a stick of wood, waiting for his sister.

8

The Defendovs were eating their evening meal. The grandmother crossed herself and sank back into her armchair. The lamp shone dimly and was unsteady. Sometimes it was turned up too high, sometimes too low. Defendov often reached out his hand to the screw; he drew it back slowly, sat back on his seat and his hand shook, not like the hand of an old man, but more as if he were raising a glass of spirits poured too full. His fingertips shook. He spoke in a clear, steady voice, as if he put his words together not with sounds but with individual letters. And he pronounced them all, even the final consonants.

The swollen neck of the lamp glowed, outlined with geranium and heliotrope tendrils. The cockroaches ran toward the warm glass, and the clock hands advanced cautiously. Time crept as it does in winter. In the room it festered; outside it congealed with a bad smell. Behind the windows, it hurried, doubled and tripled itself in the lights.

Mrs. Defendov put roast liver on the table. The soup, spiced only with onions, steamed fragrantly. Defendov talked continuously, often repeating the words "I recommend," but Zhenya heard nothing. . . . Even yesterday she had felt like crying. Now she thirsted for tears as she sat in the little jacket sewed according to her mother's instructions.

Defendov noticed how things were with her. He tried to distract her. Now he spoke to her as to a small child, then he fell into the opposite extreme. His joking questions frightened and confused her. He blindly fingered the soul of his daughter's friend, as if he were asking her heart its age. After he had detected one of Zhenya's characteristic traits, he tried to behave in conformity with it and thus help the child to stop thinking about home. But this only reminded her even more that she was among strangers.

Suddenly she could stand it no longer, got up and murmured with childish embarrassment, "Thank you. I've really eaten enough. May I look at the pictures?" Everybody looked startled and she blushed, then nodded toward the adjoining room and added, "Walter Scott. May I?"

"Go, go, my dear," said the grandmother, and with a frown at the others made them keep their peace. "The poor child," she said to her son when the claret-colored curtain closed behind Zhenya.

The grim completeness of the set of magazines, *The North*, lay so heavy upon the bookshelf that it leaned to one side, and the velvety crimson underneath had a golden luster. A pink lamp hung from the ceiling and cast no light on either of the much-rubbed armchairs. The little carpet, buried in darkness, was a surprise to the feet.

Zhenya had wanted to come into the room, sit down and cry. Tears entered her eyes but her sorrow failed to overflow. How could she shake off this sorrow, which had lain upon her like a beam since yesterday? Tears had no power over it, they could not open the sluice gates. To help them along, she tried to think about her mother.

Preparing to spend a night with strangers, she realized for the first time the depths of her attachment to this dearest and most beloved human being on earth.

Suddenly she heard Lisa's laugh behind the curtain. "Oh, you fidget, oh, you little Lisa devil," said the grandmother, coughing between her words. Zhenya wondered how she could ever have imagined that she loved this girl; her laughter sounded in the very next room, yet it was distant and useless to Zhenya. And then something turned over within her and let the tears break loose when she thought of her mother, suffering, standing among an endless row of yesterdays, as if among a crowd of people who had come to say good-by on a railway platform and remained behind when the train carried Zhenya away.

But what was really insupportable was the penetrating look Mrs. Luvers had thrown at her yesterday in the schoolroom. It had buried itself in her memory, and would now never leave her. It was an object that must be accepted, something of value to her that she had forgotten and neglected.

The wild, delirious bitterness and the utter endlessness of this feeling were so confusing that she felt she might lose her reason over it. Zhenya stood at the window and wept violently. Her tears flowed and she did not wipe them away; her hands moved, yet they grasped nothing. They reached out, clutching spasmodically, desperately and willfully.

Suddenly a thought came to her—that she was *terrifyingly* like her mother. She had the feeling with a vividness and certainty which seemed to have the power to turn the thought into reality and, through the very force of this shockingly swift conviction, make her indeed like her mother. This feeling was so sharp and penetrating that she groaned involuntarily. It was the recognition of a woman who is given the power to contemplate her external loveliness from within. Zhenya couldn't account for it to herself. It was the first time she had ever experienced anything like it. In only one particular she was not mistaken: Mrs. Luvers had once stood by a window in the same state of excitement, turned away from her daughter and her daughter's governess; she had bitten her lip and the gloved hand that clutched a pair of opera glasses.

In a stupor from weeping, but with a happy face, Zhenya went back to the Defendovs. Her walk had changed; now it was broad, dreamy and new. When Defendov saw her walk in, he realized that the picture of her that he had formed in her absence was quite inaccurate. He would have proceeded to draw another one had not the samovar interfered.

Mrs. Defendov fetched a tray from the kitchen and placed the samovar on the floor. All eyes were turned toward the wheezing copper machine, as if it were alive. Its capricious behavior was tamed when it stood at last on the table. Zhenya sat down on her chair. She decided to enter the conversation, and felt dimly that the choice of a topic was up to her. Otherwise, the others would once more leave her in her perilous solitude and not realize that her mother was present here, through her and in her. This shortsightedness on their part would hurt—and, most of all, it would hurt Mama. She addressed Mrs. Defendov, who with some difficulty was adjusting the samovar at the edge of the table: "Vassa Vassilievna . . ."

"Can you have a child?"

Lisa did not answer Zhenya at once. "Quiet, don't speak so loud. Naturally, all girls can." She spoke incoherently and in a whisper. Zhenya couldn't see her friend's face, for Lisa was looking for matches on the table and not finding any.

She knew much more about it than Zhenya; she knew *everything*, the way children know who have picked it up from the conversation of strangers. Natures whom the Creator loves rebel in such cases. They revolt and are gripped by a wild timidity. They cannot have this experience without certain pathological impulses. The opposite would hardly be considered natural: juvenile insanity bears today the seal of normality.

Somebody had once told Lisa all kinds of vulgar and filthy things in a dark corner. They didn't shock her when she heard them, and she had carried them about ever since, not forgetting one bit of the dirt that had been revealed to her. She knew it all. Her body was not surprised, her heart made no protest, her soul inflicted no punishment upon her brain because it had dared to find out without consulting her heart about things that didn't come from the soul.

"I know that." ("You know nothing," thought Lisa.) "I know that," Zhenya repeated. "I'm not asking about that. But whether one feels—you take a step and suddenly you have a child—well . . ."

"Come on," said Lisa hoarsely, repressing her laughter. "How can you yell so loud? They'll hear you!"

The conversation took place in Lisa's room. Lisa spoke so quietly that one could hear the drip from the washstand. She had found the matches, but hesitated before lighting the lamp, because she couldn't force a serious expression on her face, which was twisted into a grin. She didn't want to hurt her friend. She indulged Zhenya's ignorance because she had no idea that one could talk about these things other than in words that couldn't be used here in her home, to a friend who didn't go to school. She lit the lamp. Fortunately the pan had run over and Lisa bent down to wipe up the floor, and so she was able to conceal a new fit of laughter with her apron and the slapping of the cleaning rag. Suddenly she burst into uncontrollable laughter, for she had found a pretext: her comb had fallen into the pan.

During those days Zhenya thought of nothing but her family and waited for the hour when she would be taken home. In the morning, after Lisa had gone to high school, Zhenya dressed and went out alone.

The life of the suburb was not like life in the part of the city where she lived. Most of the day it was empty and boring here. There was nothing to please the eye. Everything one saw was good for nothing, except maybe a birch broom or a stove mop. Black slop water flowed into the street, froze instantly and turned white. At certain hours the street was crowded with very simple people. Workers crawled over the snow like cockroaches. The doors of the tea houses flew open, and waves of soap fumes rolled out, as from a laundry—as if it had turned warmer, as if spring had come, when young men ran bent over through the streets with their trousers tucked into felt boots. The pigeons had no fear of all these people. They flew back and forth above the streets, seeking food. Were any millet, oats or droppings sprinkled over the snow? A pie seller's stand gleamed in fat and warmth. This glow and warmth entered the mouths that had been scoured with cheap rotgut. The fat burned their gullets. And on the way down, some of it escaped their wheezing lungs. Was it maybe this that warmed the street?

Just as suddenly the street would become empty. Empty peasant sledges drove by, broad flat sledges with bearded men. They were sunk into their furs, which hugged their shoulders like clumsy bears. The sledges left behind sad wisps of hay and the sweet, slow-fading sound of distant sleigh-bells. The merchants disappeared at the turning behind a row of young birches, which from a distance looked like a long picket fence.

Crows came here that had flown croaking over the Luvers' house. But here they did not croak. They only let out a cry, beat their wings and perched on fences, until suddenly, as if by a sign, they flew to the trees and sat nudging one another on the bare branches. Then one feels, how late it is, how late it is in the whole wide world. So late no watch can tell the time.

Toward the end of the second week, on a Thursday, she saw him again quite early in the morning. Lisa's bed was empty. When Zhenya woke up, she heard the garden gate click shut behind her. She got up and went to the window without making a light. It was still quite dark. In the sky, in the branches of the trees and in the movements of the dogs there seemed to be the same oppressive heaviness as yesterday. This dismal weather had now lasted three days and there seemed no force that could lift it from the softening snow, as one lifts a cast-iron kettle from a rough shelf.

In the window opposite, a lamp was burning. Two bright bands of light fell beneath a horse and struck his shaggy fetlocks. Shadows glided over the snow, and then the sleeves of a ghost crossed his fur-covered arms, cast by the light flickering behind the curtain. The horse stood motionless, dreaming.

Then she saw him. She recognized him immediately from his silhouette in the window. The lame man lifted up the lamp and went out with it. The two bands of light moved behind him, became shorter, then lengthened.

The sleighs flashed into motion and even more suddenly stormed off into the darkness, as if they had gone to the steps in the rear of the house.

Strange that Tsvetkov should find her here in the suburb.

Soon the lamp reappeared and the light slid across the curtains; it began to move back again, until suddenly it came to a halt behind the curtain on the window sill, from which he had taken it.

That was on Thursday. And on Friday they finally came to take her home.

9

On the tenth day after their return, when lessons were resumed after an interruption of over three weeks, Zhenya learned the rest from her tutor.

After lunch, the doctor packed his things and left;

she asked him to say hello to the house where he had examined her in the spring, and to all the streets and the Kama. He expressed the hope that they wouldn't have to call him from Perm again. She accompanied him to the gate, the man who frightened her so much the morning after her return from the Defendovs, when Mama was asleep and she could not see her.

When she had asked the doctor what was wrong with Mama, he had started by reminding her of the night when her parents were at the theater. "After the show, they went out and the stallion—"

"Vykormish?"

"Yes, if that's his name . . . Vykormish started to lash out, reared up and trampled a passer-by."

"Trampled him to death?"

"Yes, unfortunately."

"And Mama—"

"Your Mama had a nervous shock." He smiled and tried to explain his Latin phrase, *"partus praematurus,"* in such a way that she would understand.

"And then my little dead brother was born?"

"Who told you that? Yes."

"Where? Here? Or was he already dead? No, don't tell me. Oh, how horrible! Now I understand. He was already dead, or else I would have heard him cry. I was reading into the night. I would have heard him. But when was he alive? Doctor, can such a thing be? I even went into the bedroom. He was dead. Definitely!"

What a piece of luck that she had made her observation at the Defendovs yesterday morning and that the horrible business in front of the theater happened the week before last. What a piece of luck that she recognized him yesterday. She thought confusedly that if she hadn't seen him, she would have definitely believed, after the doctor's story, that it was the lame man who had been trampled outside the theater.

And now the doctor was gone, after being their guest for such a long time, almost a member of the family. In the evening, the tutor came. It was washday. In the kitchen the linen was being put through the mangle. The hoar frost melted on the windowpanes, the garden came closer to the window, got tangled in the lace curtains, but reached as far as the table. The rumble of the mangle disturbed the conversation. Dikikh, like everybody else, thought she had changed. She noticed a change in him, too.

"Why are you so sad?"

"Do I look sad? Well, I have lost a friend."

"So you are sad, too. So many dead people—and all of them so suddenly." She sighed.

When he wanted to go on with the lesson, something inexplicable happened. Suddenly the girl began to think about how many people were dead, and the reassurance she had gained from the lamp in the room across from the Defendovs began to fade. "Wait! You were once in the tobacconist's shop, shortly before Negarat left. I saw you with somebody. Was that he?" She was afraid to say "Tsvetkov."

Dikikh was startled by the inflection in her voice. He recalled the incident and remembered that he had, indeed, been there to buy some papers and to get the collected works of Turgenev for Mrs. Luvers. Yes, that's right, he had been there with the dead man.

She jerked convulsively and tears sprang into her eyes. But she had not found out the most important thing. When Dikikh then told her, between long pauses punctuated by the creaking of the mangle, what a splendid young fellow he had been, from such a good family, he lit a cigarette. Zhenya realized that only a small hesitation stood between what the teacher was saying and what the doctor had told her. And when he had spoken a few words more, among them the word "theater," she gave a piercing scream and ran from the room.

Dikikh stood listening. There was no sound in the whole house beyond the rumbling of the mangle. He stood stiff as a stork, his neck stretched and one leg lifted to go to her aid. He went in search for the girl, believing there was no one at home and that she must have fainted. While he collided in the dark with strange objects of wood, wool and metal, Zhenya crouched in a corner and wept. He kept on searching and fumbling about, in his thoughts already lifting her unconscious body from the carpet, and winced when a tear-choked voice cried just beneath his elbow: "I'm here. Look out, there's a glass cabinet there. Wait for me in the school-room."

The curtains and the star-bright winter night outside the window reached to the floor, while at the bottom, buried to the waist in heaps of snow and dragging chains of branches over the snow, the dreaming trees lifted toward the bright light in the window. And somewhere beyond the wall, the mangle rumbled, working on bed sheets. "How can this excessive sensitivity be explained?" the teacher wondered. "Obviously the dead man had a special meaning for the girl. She's deeply upset." He had explained periodical fractions to a child; but a grown girl, almost a young woman, had sent him into the schoolroom . . . and all this in a single month? Obviously, the dead man had made a deep, inexpungible impression upon this young woman. Impressions of this kind have a name. How strange! He had given her lessons every second day and had noticed nothing. She was extremely brave, and he was deeply sorry for her. But when would she cry herself out and come in to him? Everyone was probably out. He felt genuine sympathy for her. It was a night to remember!

He was mistaken. The impression he had in mind had nothing to do with it. But he wasn't entirely wrong. The impression that was hiding behind all this in Zhenya's mind was indeed inexpungible. It was deeper even than he believed. The girl couldn't control this impression because it was important and vital to her; its importance lay in the fact that for the first time another human being had entered her life, the third person, without a name or with only a token name, who aroused neither hatred nor love, but what the Ten Commandments mean when they say: "Thou shalt not kill. . . . Thou shalt not steal. . . ." "Thou, individual and living one," they say, "shalt not do to the unknown and the other what thou dost not wish done unto thyself."

Dikikh was much mistaken when he thought that impressions of this kind have a name. They have none.

Zhenya cried because she believed she was responsible for all this. After all, she had brought him into the family on the day she had seen him in the other people's garden. And after she had unnecessarily, uselessly and senselessly noticed him, she had met him time and again, always both directly and indirectly, and against all probability, like the last time.

When she saw the book Dikikh took from the shelf she puckered her brow and declared: "No, I won't answer questions today. Put it back, please. I'm sorry. Please forgive me."

And without a word, the same hand thrust Lermontov back into the disorderly row of Russian classics.